Moses F. Sweetser

Views in the White Mountains

Moses F. Sweetser

Views in the White Mountains

ISBN/EAN: 9783337287382

Printed in Europe, USA, Canada, Australia, Japan

Cover: Foto ©Andreas Hilbeck / pixelio.de

More available books at **www.hansebooks.com**

VIEWS

IN THE

WHITE MOUNTAINS.

WITH DESCRIPTIONS

BY

M. F. SWEETSER.

PORTLAND:

CHISHOLM BROTHERS.

1879.

Electrotyped and Printed
By Rand, Avery, & Company,
117 Franklin Street,
Boston.

CONTENTS.

THE FRANKENSTEIN TRESTLE.

THE OLD WILLEY HOUSE.

Mt. Willard.   Mt. Webster.

THE WILLEY-BROOK BRIDGE.

THE GREAT CUT, WHITE-MOUNTAIN NOTCH.

Mt. Willard Range   Cherry Mt.

THE CRAWFORD HOUSE, FROM ELEPHANT'S HEAD.

THE FABYAN HOUSE.

THE PRESIDENTIAL RANGE, CAPPED WITH SNOW.

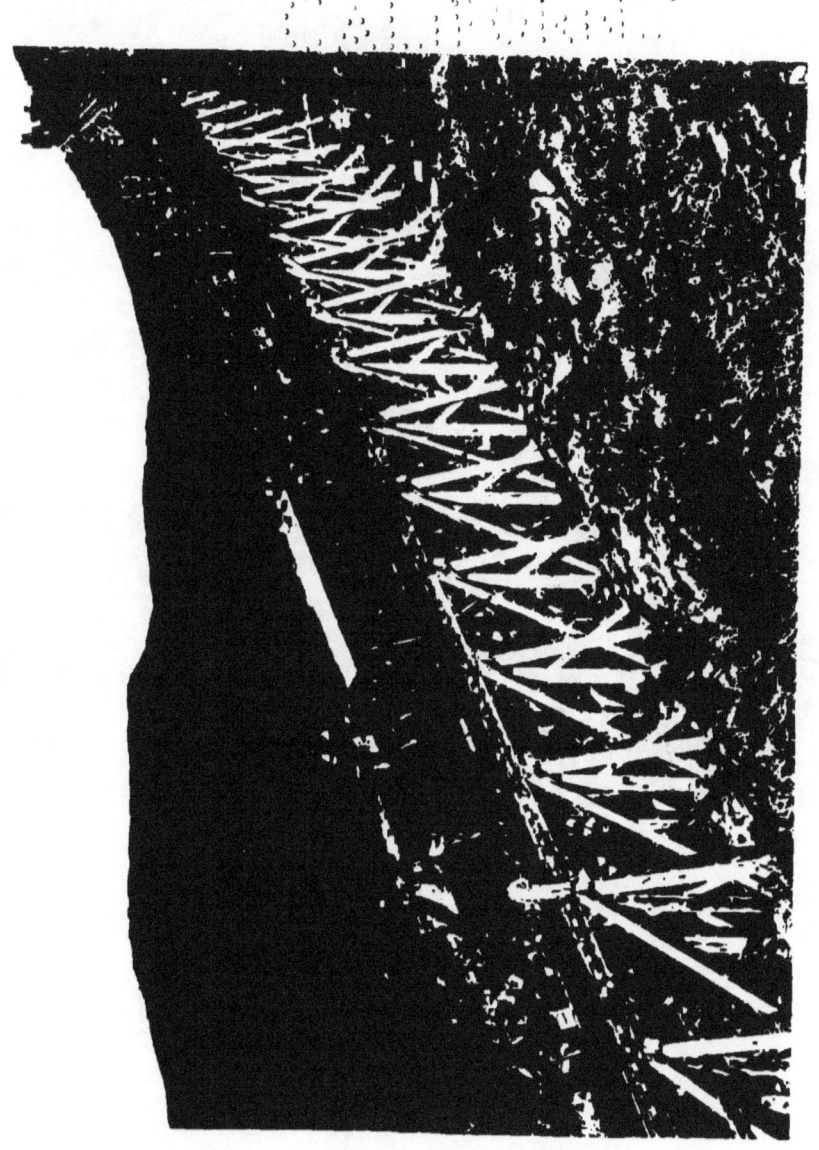

LIZZIE BOURNE'S MONUMENT, ON MT. WASHINGTON.

FRANCONIA NOTCH AND PROFILE HOUSE.

THE FRANKENSTEIN TRESTLE.

HE Frankenstein Cliff is the perpendicular rocky face of the great spur which makes out from Mount Nancy towards the Saco Valley, between the glens which shelter the Arethusa Falls and Ripley's Falls. As the train hurries northward, beyond Bemis Station, the attention is divided between the sight of this fine piece of rock-architecture and a famous view of the more distant and more imposing Mount Washington, at the head of the desolate and unvisited valley of the Mount-Washington River. But, before reaching the cliff, the railroad must cross a deep dry ravine ; and here the power of mechanical genius has manifested itself in a notable degree. The track is carried over the gulf on the celebrated Frankenstein Trestle, which is 498 feet long, and 75 feet above the rocks of the glen. The slender iron supports are firmly based on foundations of masonry, and toward the top seem more like the meshes of a spider-web than the upholding piers of a continental route. As the trains pass over the trestle, scores of heads emerge from the car-windows, looking down upon the graceful interlacings of the iron-work below, and out over the romantic glen of the Saco, inwalled by formidable mountains.

THE OLD WILLEY HOUSE.

SOON after 1770 the White-Mountain Notch was discovered by a wandering hunter, and a road was constructed through it by the authority of the State. The main route of travel between the rich farming district of Coös and the sea-coast lay through this pass, and was traversed by thousands of heavy freight-wagons every year, carrying down the farm-produce from above, and returning with supplies. In 1793 the building now known as the Old Willey House was erected, to serve as an inn for the accommodation of travellers and teamsters on this favorite route. More than thirty years later, Mr. Samuel Willey, jun., moved into the house with his family, and lived there comfortably enough until the next summer. In June, 1826, they were startled by a slide of rock and earth, which descended from the mountain, and ran over the road within sight of their windows.

Several weeks of drought ensued, baking the soil of the ridge to powder, and destroying the cohesive vitality of the herbage. Then came the storm, filling the Notch with roaring floods, illuminating the dread August night with sheets of lightning, and causing the hills to tremble with the crash of thunder-peals and the long roll of the falling deluge. It is supposed that the rapid rise of the Saco menaced the house during the night, and

The Old Willey House.

forced the family to take refuge high up on the rugged slope of Mount Willey, whence they were unable to escape in time, when the mountain itself began to give way, and the great slide swept down upon and over them.

A traveller who forced his way through the ruins which encumbered the Notch, soon afterwards, found the Willey House deserted, with the open Bible lying upon the table, and the beds disordered as if left for a hasty flight. The alarm was given in Conway, and relatives of the family quickly came up to search for their missing kinspeople. They soon found the body of a man-servant, David Allen, near a pile of earth and broken timbers, with his clinched hands full of small limbs of trees and sticks. The remains of Mr. and Mrs. Willey were recovered soon afterwards, terribly bruised, and covered with stones and earth ; and on the next day the bodies of two of the Willey children and another hired man were found. Three of the children were buried beyond all possibility of recovery. The horses in the stable were killed ; but the cattle escaped with slight bruises : and the family dog, contused and wounded, appeared at North Conway immediately after the storm, and vainly endeavored to summon assistance ; after which he disappeared, and was seen no more.

THE WILLEY–BROOK BRIDGE.

OON after the northward-bound train passes the white walls of the Willey House, seen far below in the valley of the Saco, it reaches the ravine of the Willey Brook, a short stream which rises in the gorges of Mount Willard, and descends rapidly to the Saco. The track is carried across the narrow chasm on a lattice girder bridge of iron, one hundred and forty feet long and eighty-five feet high, and a continuous wooden trestle of similar length. Above it tower the purple cliffs of Mount Willard, crowned with myriads of harebells, and seamed by deep and marvellous flumes.

As the train sweeps around the rocky promontories beyond, a succession of charming and picturesque views is unfolded, including the profound depressions of the Saco Valley, reaching away to the far southern hills; the white veils of the Silver Cascade and the Flume Cascade, adorning the opposite mountains with their silvery shimmer; and the black waters of the Dismal Pool, silently brooding in the depths of the pass. This wide variety of scenery offers objects to interest every traveller, and calls forth continual exclamations of delight. The dark majesty of the overhanging mountains, in itself almost terrifying, is contrasted with the feminine beauty of the cascades and the wavy grace of a sea of verdure, stimulating the most pleasing and satisfactory emotions in the hearts of all beholders.

THE GREAT CUT,—CRAWFORD NOTCH.

THER routes were content to go around the mountains; but the Portland and Ogdensburg Railroad hewed its way through them. Portland deemed it important that she should have a direct freight-line from the granaries of the West to her island-strewn harbor, and with her municipal bonds hired many hundreds of mercenaries, and sent them to the mountain-region to clear and level the way. The Forest City made war upon the forest.

At last the army of wood choppers and blasters and graders were brought to a halt before the vast cliffs of Mount Willard, the only remaining obstacle between them and the Connecticut-River water shed. The attack begun at once, and for weeks the narrow pass resounded with the roar of loud explosions, as the blasting operations advanced farther and farther into the live rock. Showers of fragments shot up into the air, falling heavily into the stream of the Saco, and crushing the harebells along the slopes of the mountain. And then there came a day of triumph when the last ledges gave way; and the trains swept through a deep and level trench, curving between high walls of rugged rock.

Far below, as the cars emerge from the cut, the black waters of Dismal Pool are seen on the sunken floor of the Notch, surrounded by dense thickets, and dimly reflecting the proud peaks and ponderous ridges which tower above it. Avernus itself was not more dark, more sombre, more mournful.

THE CRAWFORD HOUSE, FROM ELE-
PHANT'S HEAD.

OOKING to the northward from the high rock of Elephant's Head, this fair scene breaks upon the view.
In the foreground is the clear mirror of Saco Lake,
the source of one of the chief rivers of New England, whose
waters ripple away through the Gate of the Notch at our feet.
The bright walls of the Crawford House rise beyond, over well-
kept lawns and amid the most charming surroundings, enjoying
the cool air of an elevation of nineteen hundred feet above the
sea, and perfumed by the fragrance of the far-reaching forests.
This is one of the most famous and luxurious of the mountain-
hotels, and accommodates over three hundred guests at one
time. The pretty little station of the Portland and Ogdensburg
Railroad, in front of the house, is the debarkation-point of
many thousands of tourists every summer. Two miles distant,
by an easy carriage-road, is the top of Mount Willard, with its
magnificent view ; and about nine miles distant, over the famous
old bridle-path which crosses a line of lofty mountains, is the
summit of Mount Washington. The wonderful cascades in the
Notch — Arethusa, Ripley's, Silver, and Flume — are accessible
from this point ; and close to the house are the forest-hidden
beauties of Beecher's and Gibbs's Falls, and the artificially en-
larged lake with its boats and piers, and the shores adorned
with landscape gardening.

THE FABYAN HOUSE.

N 1792 Capt. Eleazar Rosebrook, a Massachusetts veteran of the Revolutionary war, built a farm-house and mill near the ancient mound of the Giant's Grave ; and twenty-five years later he bequeathed the estate to his grandson Ethan Allen Crawford, the giant of the hills, whose grave and monument are now to be seen hard by. Ethan was a famous guide and hunter, and often entertained travellers at his house, and led them to the top of Mount Washington. From 1803 to 1819 he kept an inn at this point ; but the house was burned, and two others quickly met the same fate. Somewhat later, Horace Fabyan erected here the largest hotel in the White Mountains, containing a hundred rooms ; but this also was swept away by fire twenty-five years ago.

The present Fabyan House is less than ten years old, and accommodates five hundred guests. The Portland and Ogdens-burgh Railroad, and the Boston, Concord, and Montreal Railroad, form a junction in front of its long front, and make communication easy to all parts of the mountains, to the adjacent Twin-Mountain and Crawford Houses, and to the summit of Mount Washington (about ten miles distant by rail). The view of the Presidential Range from the Fabyan House is full of grandeur and impressiveness ; for the entire line of peaks appears in panoramic array, closing in the eastern horizon with a stately wall of mountains.

THE WHITE–MOUNTAIN RANGE, CAPPED WITH SNOW.

THE winter scenery of the New-Hampshire highlands has a wild Alpine beauty which merits the admiration of all lovers of Nature, and calls forth the attention of increasing numbers of tourists every year. The Fabyan Cottage is now frequently visited by mid-winter travellers, who find a new and unexpected charm in the metamorphosed mountains and streams, the snow-clad peaks, and the glacial ravines. Many are they who ascend Mount Washington at that season to visit the signal-officers upon the summit, and they report that the climb is easier then than in the heated days of summer. Others have traversed Tuckerman's Ravine when its bed was filled with compact ice, and colossal icicles draped all the adjacent cliffs.

The view in our heliotype was taken from the Ammonoosuc Valley, between the Fabyan House and the base of Mount Washington, and shows the great peaks to the eastward, clad in their shining robes of snow, and glistening in the bright winter sunlight. The line where the forest ceases is clearly perceived ; and above it rises the ghostly pallor of the sub-Alpine and Alpine regions, almost blending with the pale blue sky.

JACOB'S LADDER, — MOUNT-WASHING-TON RAILWAY.

N 1858 Sylvester Marsh of Littleton secured a charter for building a railroad of new and marvellous form up the slopes of Mount Washington ; and eight years later, after overcoming an immense amount of prejudice and derision, he began the construction of the line. In 1869 the work was finished, and the quaint little locomotives reached the top of the mountain ; the track and rolling-stock having cost $150,000. Since that time many improvements have been added, tending to increase the strength and safety of the road ; and thousands of trains have ascended the mountain, carrying all their passengers in perfect safety. The track is over three miles long, with an average grade of 1,300 feet to the mile, and a maximum grade of 1,980 feet to the mile. The ascent takes an hour and a half, and is broken by halts at the four water-tanks *en-route*. The small but very powerful locomotives are attached to the lower end of the trains, and push the cars before them ; or, in descending, steadily retard their advance. There is a central rail fitted with cogs, into which plays a heavy cog-wheel attached to the engine ; and this appliance is supplemented by several independent systems of brakes.

Jacob's Ladder, — Mount-Washington Railway.

After leaving the forests of the Ammonoosuc Valley, the train ascends through dwindling sub-Alpine thickets, and broad and magnificent views open out to the west and north-west over deep glens and countless peaks, extending far into Vermont. Jacob's Ladder is a massive and firmly-bolted trestle, 5,468 feet above the sea, and about three hundred feet long, with a height of nearly thirty feet above the rocks, and an ascent of one foot in each yard of advance. The title of this section is derived from the adjacent locality on the old Fabyan Path, where the steepest shoulder of the mountain was surmounted by a rude stairway cut in the rock for the horses' feet. Here the vegetation of Labrador is seen, reindeer-moss and saxifrage peeping up amid angular fragments of schist and granite, and overspreading the desolate ruins with rare and delicate lichens. The air which breaks over the mountain's brow, and sweeps up from the dark depths of the Gulf of Mexico alongside, is filled with arctic chill; and the blazing heats of the July lowlands are replaced by a temperature which seems borrowed from the shores of Baffin's Bay.

Wider and wider grows the horizon, and fresh legions of far-away peaks rise on every side, until the view reaches the gray Adirondacks, beyond Lake Champlain.

LIZZIE BOURNE'S MONUMENT.

FTER the train on the Mount-Washington Railway has climbed upward over Jacob's Ladder, and is moving towards the summit of the mountain on easier grades, it passes on the right a rude pyramidal cairn, from which a plain inscribed tablet projects. This pile of weather-worn fragments of rock marks the place where Miss Lizzie Bourne breathed out her last breath into the deadly chill of a night-storm.

It was on a .bright September afternoon, in 1855, that the young lady, accompanied by her uncle and his daughter, sauntered up the road leading from the Glen House toward the top of the mountain. Upon reaching the Half-way House the party resolved to ascend farther, hoping to reach the summit before night-fall. But they had not gone far before a dense frost-cloud settled down over the way, and almost congealed their blood with its penetrating chill. Appalled by this event, and stricken with panic, they soon lost the path, and spent long and weary hours in vague roaming over the sharp ledges, vainly endeavoring to reach their goal above. At last Miss Bourne's strength left her, and she sank down upon the rocks, where, at ten o'clock that night, she expired. All night long the two survivors watched by her side ; and at dawn they found that they were within thirty rods of the Summit House, which had been fatally veiled from their eyes by the cold mists of the preceding afternoon.

THE GLEN HOUSE.

THIS great palace of the wildwoods is one of the chief resorts in the New-Hampshire highlands, and is especially favored by the first families of Boston and Eastern Massachusetts. In front, across the narrow glen of the Peabody Brook, rise the five loftiest peaks of the White Mountains, — Mount Washington (6,293 feet high) on the left, with the hotel on the distant crest almost hidden by nearer shoulders and foot-hills; Mount Clay (5,553 feet), lifting its rugged humps over the head of the Great Gulf; Mount Jefferson (5,714 feet), with a ponderous and well-defined peak, more to the right; the shapely spire of Mount Adams (5,794 feet), with its graceful pyramidal shape; and the swelling dome of Mount Madison (5,365 feet), closing the line on the right. Such are the elements of the front view, which has no equal in all this region. At the rear of the hotel rise the densely-wooded heights of the Carter and Wild-Cat ranges, and the air is perfumed with the fragrance of their unbroken forests.

The Glen House is 1,632 feet above the sea, and enjoys a delicious temperature during the summer and early autumn. The most comfortable and secure of Concord stages and mountain-wagons connect it with Glen Station, fifteen and a half miles south, and about five miles from North Conway; with Gorham, eight miles north, on the Grand Trunk Railway; and with the summit of Mount Washington, eight miles away.

THE FRANCONIA NOTCH AND PRO-FILE HOUSE.

HE most beautiful view of the great western pass is obtained from over Echo Lake, with the shining surface of the lake itself in the immediate foreground, and the green sea of verdure stretching away to the southward, wave on wave, to where the slopes of the mountains seem to interlace with each other in the distance. In the midst of this rich and exuberant forest appears the Profile House, white and comely, suggesting the material triumphs of civilization which are there concentrated in the heart of the hills.

The White-Mountain Notch has a worn and ancient expression, and an appearance of decadence and weariness, as if countless convulsions had shaken and swept over it, leaving their autographs in long bare slides, heaps of ruin, burnt forests, and crumbling cliffs. But the Franconia Notch seems ever fresh and young, in perennial verdure clad, and showing its rocky foundations only in such grand and picturesque forms as Eagle Cliff and the Profile. The wide sweep of foliage is scarcely broken, save by the dimpling water-gems of the lakelets about the Profile House, which confer upon the wilderness a high adornment of landscape beauty.

THE PROFILE, FRANCONIA NOTCH.

OT far from the Profile House, at a point on the road where a guide-board directs the attention upward to the right, a wonderful view is afforded of a colossal human profile projecting from the mountain-side over a thousand feet above. It is like the face of an old man weary with weight of centuries, melancholy and haggard, and with an air of faithful and undaunted expectancy. From other points near by the expression changes into various less noble forms, including a remarkable semblance of a toothless old woman. No other phenomenon of the kind in the world is so perfect in its imitation, and myriads upon myriads of travellers have come hither to study these marvellous outlines since the days when the Indian tribes brought their rude sacrifices to the mountain's base. The choice hour for visiting the view-point is in the latter part of a summer's afternoon, when the sun has sunk behind the ridge, and forms a background of brilliant sky for the face to stand out before.

The Profile is about forty feet high, and is composed of three projecting ledges of coarse granite, near the top of Cannon Mountain. The rock is rapidly decomposing, and competent observers have predicted that the resemblance to a human face will ere long totally disappear. But its memory will be preserved for centuries in the beautiful descriptions of Hawthorne and Starr King, and in numberless pictures.

www.ingramcontent.com/pod-product-compliance
Lightning Source LLC
Chambersburg PA
CBHW061240260626
47172CB00003B/944